13 Ghosts

A Collection of Original Ghost Stories
with Suggestions for Varied Work in English

Paul Groves and Nigel Grimshaw

D1342131

Hodder & Stoughton

A MEMBER OF THE HODDER HEADLINE GROUP

British Library Cataloguing in Publication Data

A catalogue for this title is available from the British Library

ISBN 0 7131 0028 1

First published 1976
Impression number 24 23 22 21 20 19 18
Year 1999 1998 1997

Printed in Great Britain for Hodder & Stoughton Educational,
a division of Hodder Headline Plc, 338 Euston Road, London
NW1 3BH by Athenæum Press Ltd, Gateshead, Tyne & Wear

To the Teacher

We have found in conversation with other teachers and by our own experience that children like to hear about, to read, to talk about and write ghost stories. We have written here thirteen ghost stories, graded in degree of difficulty, each dealing with a different theme or type of ghost. Each is accompanied by questions which point the way to discussion and written work. The first group of questions ask directly about the story, the second contain questions of more depth and general questions arising from the story, the third look at some points of language used in the tale, and the fourth group could lead to more extended pieces of writing.

Contents

Uncle Ben's Leg

Uncle Ben had lived with us for the past five years. After the funeral, his leg was left in his bedroom. It wasn't a wooden leg. We could have managed with that. We could have chopped it up and burnt it. Uncle Ben's leg was made of old-fashioned plastic and metal. When he was alive, it creaked a bit when he walked about. Being made like that it looked like a real leg. That made it worse.

The first time, they blamed me, as usual. I swore blind I'd been fast asleep.

'Well, someone was bumping about the house in the small hours,' Mum said. I could see she didn't believe me.

When she screamed the following night, we all ran downstairs. There she was at the top of the cellar steps. And there was the leg, leaning against the cellar wall. It looked just as though it was waiting for Uncle Ben to come and put it on. She said she had heard it on the stairs and then it had been hopping and creaking about down there. Dad got her calmed down. He put the leg back in Uncle Ben's wardrobe, though the door had never closed properly. He accused Becky and me of playing tricks. But we certainly hadn't put it down the cellar.

Anyway, next night it was Dad who found it. He heard something and went to the top of the stairs.

'Oh, my God!' he shouted. We ran out. He was sitting on the top step. He'd watched the leg go bouncing downstairs. We could all hear it in the living room and the kitchen. It was bumping about. When it got quiet we went down. It was propped against a chair. I could see Dad wasn't keen but he got hold of it at last and put it back in the wardrobe. It was

1

quiet after that. In the morning Becky said she supposed it soon got tired like Uncle Ben.

So Dad took it out to the town dump. He said one of its joints gave him a nasty nip but he chucked it away. I don't know why I got up at two in the morning and went to the window. There it came, jumping along, under the yellow sodium lamps. I felt cold and sick. Still, we had to let it in. It kept kicking the back door. We were afraid of it waking the neighbours. It went back quietly enough to its wardrobe.

It was obviously looking for Uncle Ben. That was the trouble. The only good thing was that it rested during the day. We got a priest in. But it was no good. As soon as he started, it got mad. We reckoned it used its straps to open door handles. This time it didn't bother. It kicked open the wardrobe. We heard that. Then it kicked out a panel in the bedroom door and came down. It went for the priest, kicking out at him. So he stopped. When he'd gone, though, it went back to its wardrobe peacefully enough.

Last Friday we took it out to the cemetery. We buried it in a family grave. It hasn't been back since.

There's one snag. It won't find Uncle Ben. He wanted to be cremated and we respected his wishes. So it could be looking further afield. It may still be roaming at nights. It knows now he's not in our house. Maybe it's coming your way.

Think It Over

Who is telling the story?
What is he first blamed for?
Why had the leg gone down the cellar?
Who is Becky?
Why did the leg give the father a nasty nip at the town dump?
What are 'the small hours'?
Why did they not tell the neighbours about the leg?
Why did the leg not like the priest?

What might have been their reason for burying the leg in a grave?

Do You Know?

Has any relative of yours died, leaving something strange behind?

How can you tell that they live in an old-fashioned house?

How might Uncle Ben have lost his leg?

Could you have touched the leg as the father did? Explain.

Why might the father have sat down on the top stair?

Where are unwanted things usually stored in your house?

Where is your town dump? Can anyone deposit rubbish there?

What might a priest do to exorcize a ghost?

Do you think they had permission to bury the leg? From whom would you need permission to bury something in a grave?

What does 'cremated' mean?

Do you think the leg will come back?

What would you do, if you saw the leg approaching? Which is more frightening, a whole ghost, or part of one?

Using Words

What parts of the body can have artificial replacements? Make a list.

'I swore blind.' What other expressions do you know with 'blind' in them?

'In the small hours', 'at daybreak'. How many phrases can you think of which describe a time of day without giving the hour or minute?

'I could see that Dad wasn't keen.' How else could this have been put?

What other words mean 'chucked'?

What is 'Becky' short for? What other shortened names do you know?

Learn these spellings: scream quite neighbours cemetery.

Write Now

Write a poem called, 'The Cellar' or 'The Thing on the Stairs'.

Have you ever been unjustly accused of doing wrong? What happened?

Write a story in which the ghostly head of a man executed in former days tries to find its body.

What strange things have happened in your home? Make a list.

In play form write the conversation the priest might have with his bishop about his experience in the house.

What difficulties would Uncle Ben have had in life? Make a list.

The Bell

In 1859 on a windy night four men sat round a fire in the local inn. They had drunk more than was good for them.

'These are hard times,' said Ben Adam. 'I've had no work for two months and probably shall not work again until harvest!'

'I may have a job,' said his friend Leonard Tork, 'but the pay is so little. It hardly keeps me and my wife and five children.'

'My master is mean,' said Jack Hardy, 'the meanest man that walked the earth.'

'This village is finished,' said Frederick Dixon. 'I shall seek my fortune abroad soon.'

As they spoke the wind brought the sound of church bells to them.

'Old Jan Musson is ringing well tonight,' said Ben. 'Hark at his tenor bell.'

'Yes, he has good cause to,' said Len Tork. 'They say his old aunt left him five hundred pounds.'

'It's not right that one man should have all that money,' said Jack Hardy.

'I hear he carries a good bit on him as he don't trust banks and is afraid to leave it all in his cottage,' said Fred Dixon.

'I wish a bit would fall out of his pockets one night,' said Ben Adam.

'It could do,' said Fred Dixon.

'How do you mean?' asked Jack Hardy.

'If he was to fall down, like,' said Fred Dixon.

'You mean if we was to tap him on the skull?' asked Ben Adam.

'You get my meaning.'

'I want no part of it,' said Len Tork.

'Just knock him out. Where's the harm in it and who's to know? You could buy your wife and children all the clothes they need.'

'But what if we should be found out?'

'How can we? Listen.' The men bent low round the fire. The landlord, drunk himself, was asleep. 'He always comes out of church last after the bell-ringing and locking up. If we wait by the lych gate, we come up behind him and . . .'

'I agree,' said Ben Adam.

'So do I,' said Jack Hardy.

'And you, Len?'

'All right. But I hope to God it goes right.'

The four men crouched round the lych gate. The wind blew and rustled the bushes behind which they hid. The bells suddenly stopped. Len Tork found his heart beating faster. There were footsteps and laughing and joking as seven bell ringers passed through the gate.

'Not yet,' whispered Fred Dixon.

They waited another five minutes. Then more footsteps were heard coming down the church path.

'It's him,' said Ben Adam.

The four men gripped lengths of wood and stones.

'Now!' yelled Fred Dixon.

Jan Musson was knocked and beaten to the ground. Fred Dixon went through his pockets, ripped through the lining of his clothes and found three hundred pounds.

'What did I tell you?' he said, money spilling out of his fingers.

'We've killed him,' said Leonard Tork.

'Nonsense,' said Ben.

As he said this the moon came from behind a fast-moving cloud. Jan Musson opened one bloodstained eye and looked at the four faces peering at him. 'A curse on you all,' he said. Then he died.

The murder was not solved. The four men explained their new-found wealth by saying they had won it at the races. Some of the villagers were suspicious, but no shred of evidence could connect them with the murder. The landlord of the inn had cleared them by saying they were with him all night.

So they enjoyed their money till harvest time, when one day Ben Adam was working on top of a corn rick stacking the corn with his pitchfork. Suddenly he stopped. 'Who is bell-ringing at this time?,' he asked.

'That's Jan Musson's tenor bell,' said his fellow worker.

'He's dead,' said Ben Adam.

'That's the bell he used to ring.'

The bell rang for half an hour. As it rang Ben Adam became more and more agitated. 'I wish that damn bell would stop,' he said.

'It's loud today,' said his fellow worker.

Suddenly Ben Adam gave a cry and ran round the top of the rick shouting, 'The bell! The bell! The bell!' Then he slipped and fell off the rick on to his own pitchfork. He died slowly from stomach wounds, saying, 'The bell. The bell. The be . . .'

Meanwhile the Vicar had got to the church just as the bell stopped. The bell rope was swinging but no one was there.

Leonard Tork drank a great deal of his money. One night he was at the inn when the tenor bell started to ring.

'That's Jan Musson's bell,' said someone.

'Don't say that!' said Len Tork. He went white.

'It's ringing like when Ben Adam died.'

'No,' said Tork.

'We must go and fetch the Vicar,' they said.

Leonard Tork was left alone with the landlord. 'We was here when Musson died,' shouted the terrified Tork. 'You said so.'

'That's right,' said the landlord.

'The bell!' said Len Tork. 'Why can't it stop ringing? The

bell. The bell.' He staggered out of the inn. As he reached the bridge he slipped and fell in the river. The river was full after heavy rain and his drunken struggles were not strong enough to reach the bank. He drowned, fighting and struggling.

As the Vicar and the men entered the church the ringing stopped, but the bell rope was still swinging. They stood and watched.

Jack Hardy and Fred Dixon met in Dixon's cottage.

'I tell you,' said Hardy, 'Jan Musson's spirit has got Ben and Len. We must get away from here.'

'We must. They say he acted very strange last night. He might have let something slip.'

They fled the village and were not seen there again.

A year later two figures could be seen in the outback in Australia.

'We did well in leaving England,' said Fred Dixon.

'We did,' said Jack Hardy. 'I reckon that gold strike of ours will make us millionaires.'

'We must get back and stake our claim.'

'Gold! Gold! Gold!' shouted Jack Hardy.

'Gold! Gold! Gold!' sang Fred Dixon.

Their shouts echoed in the mountain.

'Gold! Gold! Gold!' came back the sound.

'Did you hear that?' asked Fred Dixon. He had stopped and gone pale.

'What?' asked Jack Hardy.

'A bell.'

'It was the echo.'

'No, it's a bell.'

They listened. Slowly and clearly, across the Australian wastes, came the sound of Jan Musson's tenor bell.

'Run!' shouted Fred.

They ran and in the dusk light sank into a bog. Their death was slow and terrible as the bog crept over their heads choking them with mud and slime.

At that moment back in England, the Vicar and some villagers had burst into the church. In the bell tower a grey figure had just stopped pulling the rope. It turned and smiled at them. It had the face of Jan Musson. Then it disappeared. No one will touch that tenor bell to this day.

Think It Over

What was Ben Adam's work?

Why did Leonard Tork not complain to a trade union about his pay?

Who is the ring-leader of the men? Who understands him first? Who seems the least evil of the men? How do you know?

How do you know that Jan Musson does not trust banks?

Why might the landlord have said that they were with him all night?

What is it that makes Ben Adam so agitated when the bell rings?

What is the outback in Australia?

How did Fred and Jack get rich?

Why was the sound of the bell even stranger in the Australian outback?

Why would the bell never ring again? Would you touch the tenor bell? Why?

Do You Know?

Why is the date given? When was gold discovered in Australia?

What other kinds of bells are there beside the tenor?

What is a cornrick? Why are there so few of them nowadays? Where might you still see them?

What is a lych gate?

Why did the men decide to fetch the Vicar when the bell rang so strangely?

Why was the figure in the church grey?

Using Words

'As they spoke the wind brought the sound of church bells to them.'

Complete these sentences. They need not have anything to do with the story:

As he listened . . .

As she waited . . .

As the sound of hooves came nearer . . .

They stood by the wall as . . .

He slowly realized the truth as . . .

'Windy.' Write down ten words to describe various weather conditions. You could draw a little picture to illustrate each one.

'Tap him on the skull' is a polite way of saying something blunt or unpleasant. Give a polite way of saying:

The car crashed into the tree.

I had the guts ache this morning.

There was a horrible stink coming from the room.

What sayings do you know with the word 'moon' in them?

'Terrified Tork.' How many words that make sense beginning with the same letter can you put together? (There are many tongue twisters like this.)

What is the word for bell-ringing? It begins camp . . .

Have you noticed how conversation is written with a new line for each speaker? Write out this conversation correctly and then check it against the book:

it could do said Fred Dixon how do you mean asked Jack Hardy if he was to fall down like said Fred Dixon.

'Ben Adam became more and more agitated.' Suggest three

words which, like 'agitated', tell you about Ben Adam's state of mind.

Learn these spellings: month   length   through   probably

Write Now

Write the conversation in play form that the Vicar might have had with the other people in church when they saw the bell rope swinging for the second time.

What happened to Len Tork's wife and children? Write the story as if you were Mrs Tork.

Draw a plan of a typical English village.

In this village you might have many tradesmen. Find out and write about these: the blacksmith, the wheelwright, the baker, the miller and the carrier.

What sounds frighten you? Do any particular sounds have memories for you? Or write a poem called 'The Wind at Night'.

The Hands

Edward Dobbs was a rich man. He was thought to be a millionaire. But how rich he really was could not be known because Mr Dobbs never told anybody. As well as being a rich man he was also a recluse—a man who lives shut away from the world. Indeed, with some of his money he had bought an old castle. The castle was on an island in Scotland and could only be reached by small boat. People also kept away from it because it was thought to be haunted.

How Mr Dobbs had got his millions was not very clear. It was known that he started life as a poor man. He was the son of a milkman and he was born in the back streets of Liverpool. In his early life he had worked on a market stall. Then he went away for many years and he returned to England a rich man. Some said he had been to South Africa; others said to South America. But wherever it was there were strong rumours that he had found silver and opened a mine. He had got rich by working his miners like slaves. Another rumour said that over a hundred native miners had been killed in his mine because of the bad conditions. The number was exact: one hundred and thirty.

He had no friends and he talked to no one except Mr Stone. Mr Stone was his servant. He was a very old man who had lived all his life in the castle. When Mr Dobbs bought the castle it was a condition that he should keep on Stone. They spoke few words to each other. Dobbs growled out his orders and Stone, saying little, went about his work slowly.

As soon as he was in the castle, Dobbs went about cutting himself off from the rest of the world. He forbade all visitors. The boat was to call once a month to leave food and oil on the

13

quay to be fetched by Stone. No one was to approach the castle. Then he took his final step. He had all his money shipped from the bank, in silver coins, to the island. He distrusted paper money and he also knew it would be difficult to rob him of the heavy silver.

He instructed Stone that the money should be put in the Green Room.

'The Green Room?' asked Stone. 'Did you say the Green Room?'

'Yes, the Green Room, Stone.'

'I wouldna advise the Green Room.'

'Why not?'

'I canna say.'

'Then put it in there.'

'They will be upset.'

'Who will be upset?'

'I canna say.'

'I own this castle. Get out and put the money in the Green Room.'

Stone slowly worked for many days to stack the money, which was in bags, in the Green Room. All the while he muttered to himself: 'The man's a fool; it should not be in the Green Room.' He also took good care not to work after sunset.

It took several weeks to stack the money in the room. Some of it was piled to the ceiling. Dobbs then moved in. He was a miser who wished to practise his craft. The only time he was not to spend counting his money was when he ate and slept. Stone was banned from the room now, though outside he was to leave food and drink.

That night, by the light of a dim oil lamp, Dobbs began to count his money. His heart raced at the sight of it all and he longed to feel every silver piece in his fingers.

He counted till midnight when he planned to rest in a chair. Suddenly the air grew chill. The hair rose on the back of Dobb's neck and he went rigid as two arms came round his body to make four hands on the table. With a great effort he turned his stiff body. Nobody was there. The arms were attached to nothing.

Despite his fear he became fascinated by the hands. They were scarred, like a miner's, with blue scars. They fumbled clumsily with the money in front of them. Fumbling and dropping the coins, they put them into piles of one pound. When they had counted out ten piles they disappeared. Dobbs called for Stone, but he did not come. Dobbs did not sleep that night but sat staring at the table.

The same thing happened the next night. As midnight had finished striking, the hands appeared. Again Dobbs stopped counting and watched, fascinated, the fumbling fingers. Another ten pounds was counted out. Again he did not sleep.

Stone noticed that little of the food had been touched.

The hands counted the money for twelve nights. Then on the thirteenth night they stopped. Dobbs saw that there were one hundred and thirty piles on the table. Slowly the hands left the table and came for Dobb's throat. He struggled and cried out for Stone but the hands gripped and gripped and choked him. He struggled away from the table but the hands clung to him and would not let go. He jumped about and tried to scream but as his own hands reached the door knob his last breath was choked from him.

After some days, Stone, noticing the food had not been touched, went in and found his master slumped by the door. 'I told him not the Green Room,' he said.

The Coroner returned a verdict of death from natural causes.

A solicitor going through Dobb's papers noted that the funeral had cost one hundred and thirty pounds.

Think It Over

When do you first realize that Dobbs was neither friendly nor talkative?

What made his castle difficult to reach?
Why would it have been difficult to steal the money?
Why was Stone careful not to work in the Green Room after sunset?
Why did Dobbs keep Stone out of the room?
Would you say Dobbs was brave?
To whom might the hands have belonged?
Why did the hands fumble?
Why was the coroner's verdict not one of murder or why was Stone not suspected of murder?
What was odd about the funeral?

Do You Know?

Can you name a millionaire? If you earned a million a year how much would you get each week? What would you do with it?
Have you ever visited any Scottish islands? Name an island where this story might have taken place.
What is supposed to be haunted in your neighbourhood?
Name a successful person who was born in poor conditions.
How might the miners have been killed?
In which country did Dobbs probably have his mine?
Why might Dobbs have been to blame for the death of his miners?
Silver money would be difficult to steal. Why else did Dobbs like having his money in silver?
Why should he have been haunted by a pair of hands?
Could you have turned your body if the hands came round it?
What things are supposed to happen at midnight?
What is a coroner? What is the name of the coroner in your town?

Using Words

A word which means a man who lives entirely alone in the wilds is her . . .

What part of the British Isles might Stone come from? How can you tell? Which is your favourite dialect?

Without changing the order of the letters, how many shorter words can you get out of 'fascinated'?

Punctuate this by looking back at the story:

the green room asked stone did you say the green room yes the green room stone i wouldna advise the green room why not i canna say then put it in there

Avarice (greed for wealth) is one of the seven deadly sins. Can you name any others?

Complete these sentences. They need not have anything to do with the story:

He kept away from there because . . .

He bought an old house because . . .

She always went there because . . .

Because he was old . . .

Because there were so many of them in the boat . . .

Learn these spellings: because several fascinated stopped

Write Now

You are riding your bike when two other hands grasp the handlebars and . . .

In play form write down what the miners might say about Mr Dobbs.

Write a poem called 'The Miser' or 'The Island' or 'The Locked Room'.

What was the reason for Stone's dislike of the Green Room?

Who were 'They'? Write the story behind this mystery in the castle.

Draw a diagram of the castle or of a mine.

The Baby Sitter

Mandy had blue eyes and brown hair. She looked gentle and kind. People liked to have her baby-sitting for them. Inside, Mandy was different. She did not like babies. But she liked baby-sitting. She liked the power it gave her. She would say to the children, 'Do you want a story?' and when they said, 'Yes,' she would tell them a ghost story. She liked watching their faces when they listened. Perhaps later, she thought, they would have nightmares. None of the children told their parents about the ghost stories. Mandy warned them against it. She said, if they told, real ghosts would come in and get them.

That night she stood in the living room. Her kind, gentle eyes were fixed on Mrs Nightwalk's face. Mandy was listening carefully and politely. Mrs Nightwalk had green eyes and long red hair. She wore a long dress. There was no Mr Nightwalk.

'There's some food in the fridge—ice-cream,' said Mrs Nightwalk. 'And there's some cake in a tin. I've put coffee, milk and sugar on the table. Help yourself. I'll pay you when I get back. It may be late.'

'That's all right,' said Mandy.

'He's upstairs in bed,' said Mrs Nightwalk. 'He's a good boy. He won't be any trouble.'

'No,' said Mandy.

'I must be off now,' said Mrs Nightwalk. 'Watch television, if you like.'

'I'll go up and see him first,' said Mandy. 'Maybe he wants a story.'

'Just as you like,' said Mrs Nightwalk. 'Goodnight.'

'Goodnight,' said Mandy. She went upstairs, smiling to herself.

'Hello,' she said to the little boy. He had a funny face. It looked old. His eyes were wide and brown. They looked frightened already. Mandy smiled at him. He had red hair, too.

'Would you like a story?' she asked.

'Mm.' He nodded.

'I'll just put this big light out,' said Mandy. 'It's better with only the light from the landing. Wait until I've got a chair.'

She turned out the big light and drew a chair to the bed. 'Ready?' she whispered.

'Yes,' said the little boy.

'Well, then—' said Mandy. 'There was once a man who lived by a graveyard.' She watched his face. Again she smiled to herself. 'People said that there was treasure in the graveyard. They did not know where it was. But the man thought he knew. One night, at midnight, he went into the graveyard. He took a spade and he began to dig. He dug and dug until his spade hit wood. It was the lid of coffin. He uncovered the coffin and opened it. He held the lamp high. There was no treasure and he threw the spade down angrily. But the coffin was not empty. There was a skeleton in it. The man took out the skull and looked at it. 'I'll take this,' he said. 'Better than nothing. Perhaps someone might buy it.' He put the lid back on the coffin and filled in the grave. Then he brushed the earth off the skull and examined it. Its empty eyes looked back at him. He went home, put away his spade and hid the skull under his bed. Then he went to sleep.

He was sleeping soundly the next night, when something woke him. He sat up on his elbow. The room was full of moonlight. The clock told him that it was midnight again. He listened.

Something was scratching at the door of his cottage. Then the latch lifted and he heard the door creak open. Something rattled on the stone floor of the kitchen. It sounded like a footstep. The steps slowly crossed the kitchen. He heard the first stair creak. Then he heard the voice. 'Give me my bone!' it cried. The blind footsteps made the second stair creak. And then the third.

'Give me my bone!' the dry voice cried again. The footsteps came higher. The man lay flat in bed and pulled the clothes over his head. The steps were outside his bedroom door. 'Give me my bone!' wailed the voice. The man heard a creak. His door had opened. The footsteps shuffled in. 'Give me my bone!' was loud in the man's ears. He heard the footsteps come across to his bed. They were beside the bed. 'Give me my bone!'

Then bony fingers dug into the man's arm and the thing called. 'Ah! Here it is!' The skull rattled under the bed.

Mandy stopped and laughed aloud. When she had said, 'Ah! Here it is!' she had grabbed the little boy's arm. He had jumped in the bed and shouted. Now he lay there and stared at her. He was far too frightened to speak.

'Did you like that story?' asked Mandy. 'Shall I tell you another one?' Then the smile left her face. There was something else in the room. It slithered and rustled. There was more than one strange thing in the room with them. Up near the ceiling, in a dark corner, something stirred. Then it fluttered like a bat. A cobweb brushed across her face; something slid over her foot. A white shape grew in another corner. Then, quite clearly in her ear, a deadly voice whispered. 'Now, I'm going to eat you up.'

With a scream Mandy ran from the room, down the stairs and out into the street. She did not stop until she got home. Even in her own bed she still shivered. The things in the little boy's bedroom seemed still with her.

Later, Mrs Nightwalk came home. She closed the front door and went upstairs. The little boy was awake in the darkness. The room was quiet and peaceful.

'You ought to be asleep,' said Mrs Nightwalk. 'It's after

midnight.'

'In a minute,' said the little boy. 'I'm thinking.' He smiled.

'Has Mandy gone already?' asked Mrs Nightwalk.

'She has,' said the little boy.

'But I didn't pay her,' said Mrs Nightwalk.

'I paid her,' said the little witch-boy to his witch-mother.

Think It Over

Why did Mandy like baby-sitting?

Why did the children not tell their parents about Mandy's stories?

What preparations did Mandy make to be sure that the story would be more frightening?

What clues are there that the mother and the boy are not ordinary people?

Why did the footsteps 'rattle' across the floor of the kitchen?

What did Mandy do as the story ended to make sure that the boy was really frightened?

What sort of an expression was there on her face when the story finished?

What was it, perhaps, that frightened Mandy in the witch-boy's bedroom?

What made Mandy shiver in bed?

What does the last sentence of the story mean?

Do You Know?

How would you describe Mandy's character?

Why did Mandy not mind if Mrs Nightwalk came home late?

Why did she agree when Mrs Nightwalk said the little boy would be no trouble?

What prevented the man in Mandy's story from running away?

What made Mandy laugh?

What sort of things slither?

Are ghost stories suitable for young children? Why?

What was the last nightmare you had?

What do people leave for you to eat when you baby-sit?

When do people smile to themselves?

What stories frightened you as a child?

Did you ever run home frightened as a child? If so, for what reason?

On what night are witches supposed to ride on broomsticks?

Using Words

'She liked watching their faces when they listened.' Complete these sentences. They need not have anything to do with the story.

She liked watching their faces when . . .

I'll pay you when . . .

He was sleeping soundly the next night when . . .

When the cage door opened . . .

When the bus arrived, to his surprise . . .

You could call what happened to Mandy 'The biter . . .'

The footsteps of the ghost in the story 'rattle' across the floor. Put three words in these sentences which suggest the kind of sound made:

The old man's footsteps . . . in the lane.

She heard the feet of the little boy as they . . . up the steps.

The . . . of the horses' hooves came to their ears.

'Scratch'. How many other words can you find which imitate a small but repeated sound?

Learn these spellings: listened   creak   heard   frightened

Write Now

Give an account of where Mrs Nightwalk might have been and what she had been doing on that particular evening.

Write a poem called 'The Creaking Stair' or 'The Shadows in the Corner of the Bedroom'.

Write out three creepy sentences from the story. Then make up three of your own.

Describe a witch.

Make a list of the special things you might find in a witch's refrigerator.

Write a story in which you are baby-sitting when there is a tap at the window.

Write in play form the conversation Mrs Nightwalk might have with another witch she meets on her night out.

Draw the grave robber at work or the thing Mandy saw in the bedroom.

Give an account of an evening's baby-sitting you have done.

The Cottage in the Woods

John was a good runner. He was not a fast runner, but he could run a long way. So he became a cross-country runner at school.

One day he was out on a training run when he decided he needed some practice in running up and down hills. He left the proper school route by the river and cut off into the Dunstone Woods. He had run along a path through tall trees for about half a mile when he came to a wide ditch. There were big stones on the other side but he thought that with the speed he was running downhill he could leap it and land on a patch of mud. He leapt and slipped, and his head banged against a stone.

But he was all right and he picked his way up the stones to the top of the bank. As he scrambled over the top he saw a cottage in front of him. At the gate stood a lady in an apron. She was beckoning to him. John ran up to her and stopped, panting. There was something old-fashioned in her clothing. But his mind was taken off this by the distress of the lady. 'I have to fetch a doctor to my husband,' she said. She was white and shaking. 'Will you please look after my cat till I get back? She is so ill.'

It seemed an odd request but he could not refuse. 'Sure,' he said. The lady showed him into a dark room. The room, like the lady, was old-fashioned. On a chintz sofa in a basket was a large black cat. 'Please give her a drink if she needs it. My poor Aggy.'

Still trembling, she left him. John looked through the window and saw her get on a very old bicycle and ride away. He then looked round the room. A pendulum clock ticked away on the mantlepiece which was draped with green material. The shelf was filled with ornaments, many of which were pottery cats. Coal was burning in the grate, but it gave out no heat that he could feel. On the wall were many old prints and photographs. The calendar struck him as odd: it was for 1921. He thought she must have kept it for the picture.

The time ticked away. John became bored. He hoped the lady would be back soon. The cat was obviously very ill. He tried to give it a drink but it would not take it. As he put the saucer back on the table, he heard a low moan. His heart beat faster. Then he remembered the lady's husband. He must be upstairs. He was not alone.

The low moan came again on an eerie wind which had now got up. It still frightened him although he thought he knew the cause of it. The man was obviously in a lot of pain.

Then the moans came more quickly: 'Oo . . . oo . . . oo . . . oo.' Perhaps the man was dying and needed help. But he had never seen a dying man. He would have no idea how to help. The wind rose and the moans came again. He would have to do something. He looked out of the window in the hope that the lady had returned with the doctor. The sun had gone down and it was rapidly getting dark. He sat down again on the edge of the sofa. 'Oo . . . oo . . . oo . . . oo.' The moans were louder this time. He would have to go upstairs and see if he could help.

The stairs led off a dark hallway. He could find no light switch to give him comfort. He climbed the stairs slowly. They were narrow and creaked.

He found himself on a landing with three doors leading off it. With a trembling hand he opened the first one and peeped round it. The room was empty. He opened the next. The room was empty again. 'Oo . . . oo . . . oo . . . oo.' Yes, the moans came from the door at the end of the landing. He opened the door quickly. And there on the floor a man was lying covered in blood. Stuck in his head was an axe.

As John looked he gave a low moan. Then his mouth

sagged open, the jaw dropped, and the blood-covered eyes stared at him.

John reached the bottom of the stairs in two leaps. Then he was out of the door running, running, running, trying to get away but not moving forward. Then he was falling . . . falling . . . falling . . . .

He found himself at the bottom of the ditch in two or three inches of water. He slowly picked himself up. He felt a little dizzy, but he was otherwise all right. He climbed out to take his bearings. Then he remembered the cottage. He looked. It was not there. The cottage where he had seen the man with the axe in his head was not there. It must have been a dream. But how? Had he knocked himself out on the stones? Slowly he jog-trotted back through the wood to school.

'Where on earth have you been?' asked the PE Master. 'I've been waiting two hours for you. I've had parties out looking for you. I was just about to send for the police.'

'I went to jump this ditch, sir . . .'. John told his story.

The PE master was impatient at first but, as John went on with the story, he listened with mouth open. 'How strange,' he said, at the end. 'Look, I want you to write down what happened to you, word for word so you don't forget the details, when you get home. Then I want you to bring it to school tomorrow.'

The history master looked at John. 'You're pulling my leg,' he said.

'No, sir. It's the truth.'

'Well, it's very odd, very odd.'

'What is, sir?'

'Never mind.'

In the staff room the two masters were talking.

'Do you know, you were right. He told me in detail, even to

the right time, a description of the murder done in 1921 at the cottage in Dunstone Woods. The classic case of the woman who murdered her husband with an axe because she thought he had poisoned her cat. The cottage burned down in 1923.'

'I thought you would be interested,' said the PE master.

'Now, could he have read it in an old paper?'

'He's a very truthful boy.'

'He is.'

'And, do you know, I went out looking for him myself and I jumped the ditch by Dunstone Cottage ruins. He wasn't there.'

'It gets more curious.'

'What shall we say to him?'

'Nothing.'

'Nothing?'

'Yes, he's a good boy, and I think some things are best left alone.'

'Perhaps you're right,' said the PE master.

Think It Over

What was the first odd thing that John noticed about the old lady?

What odd request did she make?

What clues about a time past are there in the room?

What was strange about the fire?

How long had he apparently been in the cottage when he heard the moans?

What surprises you most in the story?

How long might he actually have been missing?

Why did the PE master ask John to write out what happened to him?

What made the masters feel that John really had seen the cottage?

Do You Know?

When is the cross-country season?
Who do you think is Britain's best long distance runner?
What sort of running ability are you training for by running up and down hills?
Why were the boys supposed to keep to a route?
What is the oddest thing you have been asked to do?
How can you tell direction in a wood without a compass?
If you wanted to find out something about your local history, where would you go?
Has anything that happened in your area been mentioned in the national news?
When was the death penalty for murder abolished?
What do you think is the most famous murder case?
Why do you think the history master decided to say nothing to John?

Using Words

'It still frightened him although he knew the cause of it.'
Complete these sentences. They need not have anything to do with the story:
He walked to school although . . .
She did not believe her although . . .
Many people were there although . . .
Although he was only fifteen . . .
Although he had been to prison . . .
'Chintz' is a furnishing fabric. Name some others.
How many words for ditch do you know? (They vary in different parts of the country.)
Give another word for 'eerie'.
Give another title for the story.
Write out the 1921 paper headline for the murder.
'Scrambled'. How many words can you get out of this (a) by

29

not altering the order of the letters, (b) by altering the order?

Write Now

Write a murder story in which the murderer is caught by a mistake he or she makes.

Write a poem called 'The Lonely Runner' or write how it feels to run cross-country.

Imagine a map of the places in the story and then draw it.

Write a story about a man who hates cats.

Write a story which begins: 'It was midnight. The trees creaked in the eerie wind. He heard a low moan . . .'

In play form write down the quarrel that led up to the murder.

Make a list of the things you would expect to find in a room about fifty years ago.

Freddie Tompkins

'Sit up straight! Hands behind your backs! When I say sit up straight, hands behind your backs, I want to see forty-eight backs as straight as this rule and forty-eight pairs of hands held as tight as knots. You, boy, what do you think you are doing?

Freddie Tompkins made no reply. He could not get any words to come out of his mouth which was as dry as sawdust. He had come to the board school in Stepney the day before. His family had had to move from a small village near Colchester. He had been happy in the village school. It had been run by an old lady called Miss Griggs and there was just one class of twenty pupils, and he knew them all down to the youngest. Here, in London, the school was bigger than his village church and he knew no one.

'Speak out clearly, boy! Didn't they teach you to speak in Essex? Was it a dame school or a dumb school you went to?'

The class laughed. The master smirked, pleased at his wit. Then he bent down so that his face was three inches away from Freddie's and all Freddie could see were small pupils behind pebble glasses.

'A pupil who does not speak when spoken to is guilty of dumb insolence, boy.'

Miss Griggs had never shouted at him or made him sit up till his back ached. She was firm, but kind with it. She had often given him sweets for good work.

'I was try . . . I was trying . . . I was trying to sit up, sir.'

'Then your trying is not good enough, boy. We have the Inspectors coming and they don't want to see you flopping around like a stale Essex cabbage.'

More laughter.

'Come out to the front and look at the rest of the class. See how we sit up in Stepney.'

Freddie Tompkins edged out of the fixed bench trying not to touch his strange neighbours.

'Hurry up, boy!' The master cut him twice across the legs with his cane. Forty-seven pairs of eyes ate into his burning skin.

'Sit up straight, class. Straight! That's how it's done, Tompkins. You can't even stand up straight, boy. Hands behind your back, head up. Not like an Essex goose, boy. Stick your chin in. I've got the Inspectors coming and they don't want to see you slummocking about in the classroom. Now, back to your bench.'

Freddie Tompkins thought of the old school; just one classroom and the stove they crouched round in winter. He thought too of the meadows surrounding the school and the walks across the marshes to the open sea. Stepney was like being shut up in a barn. He had walked in the middle of the road coming to school, for fear of some of the buildings falling on him.

'Now, I want you to write the date on your slates. The 12th of October, 1880.'

They had come to Stepney because his father had the chance of a job in the furniture factory. Once harvest had finished in Essex there was no work to be had till the spring.

'Neat, copperplate writing. The Inspectors won't want to see a lot of scribble. Hold yours up, Tompkins. What do you call that, boy?'

'The . . . the . . . the date, sir.'

'Come out here at once.' The master cut him again across the legs as he came out. 'Tompkins is going to show us his apology for handwriting.'

He felt faint. He tried to focus on a knot of wood in the floor.

'Tompkins can't look us in the face, can he?'

The knot of wood became a whirlpool. He fell, hitting his head on the corner of the front bench.

'Miss! Miss!'

Miss Griggs looked up from correcting a sum. In the doorway was Freddie Tompkins caught in a shaft of sunlight.

'Why, Freddie! I didn't know you had moved back to the village. What's the matter? Didn't your father get the job?'

Freddie Tompkins smiled at Miss Griggs. He held out a hand towards her as if trying to show her something. Then he turned and walked out of the door.

'Freddie, come back. Harold, run after him and see what's the matter.'

Five minutes later Harold Thorpe returned breathlessly. 'I can't see him anywhere, Miss. He's just vanished.'

'How strange,' said Miss Griggs. 'I never knew his family were back.'

'Their cottage was empty this morning, Miss,' said Lilian Turner.

'He's dead, sir.'

'Nonsense!,' said the master. 'He's just gone into a faint.' He slapped Freddie on the face.

'He's a funny colour, sir.'

'Get me some water, boy.'

'What's wrong here?' The Headmaster walked in.

'This boy has fainted, sir,' said the master, though he did not look so certain now. Sweat oozed from his upper lip. 'Probably had no breakfast.'

'What's this wound in his head, Hodgson?'

'He hit the bench, sir, as he fell.'

'What was he doing out of his desk?'

'I had had to reprimand him, sir, for bad work.'

'I can feel no pulse, Hodgson. We must send for a doctor at once.'

The coroner returned a verdict of accidental death. No blame was attached to the master for, as the Headmaster explained to the coroner, Hodgson was his best master and had many good reports from the Inspectors.

Think It Over

How do you know it is a schoolmaster talking?

How soon do you know that the story does not take place at the present time?

Where is Freddie when the story begins?

Why do the class laugh?

Why does the master mention cabbages and geese? What is he implying?

How can you tell that the buildings were high and the streets were narrow in Stepney?

What did Freddie's father work at in Essex?

Why did the knot of wood become a whirlpool?

When do you know that Freddie is dead?

What might he be trying to show Miss Griggs?

Why were the children and teacher not frightened of the ghost?

Why does the Headmaster think that Hodgson was one of his best masters?

What does it tell you about the kind of school it was?

Do You Know?

In how many ways does discipline in your school differ from that of the board school in Stepney?

How much bigger is the class compared to your form or group?

What county is Colchester in?

Why are pebble glasses so called? What does it tell you about the schoolmaster's sight?

What makes you work best: fear of punishment; or reward?

Where is Stepney?

What is a fixed bench?

How was the heating in the Essex school different from that in schools today?

Why did they write on slates?

Have you ever had the Inspectors in your school? What is their job?

What should you do if you feel faint?

Was the Coroner's verdict the right one in your opinion?

Using Words

'Sit up straight!', 'Hands behind backs!' A command has an exclamation mark behind it. Make up three of your own commands and remember the exclamation mark each time.

'As tight as knots', 'as dry as sawdust'. How would you describe tight and dry? As tight as . . . As dry as . . .

'Slummocking' What might this mean? It is probably not in your dictionary so you will have to guess it.

'Dumb insolence.' What might this mean?

'He held out his hand towards her, as if trying to show her something.'

Complete these sentences. They need not have anything to do with the story:

He ran from school as if . . .

His face was bleeding as if . . .

Her cakes tasted as if . . .

The prisoners looked as if . . .

As if in a dream he . . .

'He's a funny colour, sir.' What do we mean by 'funny'?

Dame school—dumb school. Do you know any jokes in which there is a play on words?

What is the word meaning fear of being shut in? It begins
claus . . .

Mr Hodgson calls Freddie 'boy'. Who would call him Freddie? Who might call him Frederick or Tompkins?

What are you called (a) in school by teachers, (b) by your
friends, (c) at home, (d) by a stranger in the street?

Write Now

Write a story in which someone who is killed in an air crash
appears at the time of the crash in a different place.

In play form write a conversation Miss Griggs and the
children of the Essex school might have when they hear of
Freddie's death.

Write a poem called 'Tall Buildings' or 'The Lonely Marshes'
or 'Was It a Ghost?'.

Imitate copperplate handwriting if you can find an example
in an old book or document. Copy out part of the story in
it.

How might the day in the Stepney School be different from
the day in your school? List some of the differences.

Write a story in which a ghost makes someone change his
ways.

Have you ever moved to a new school? Describe what the first
day felt like and what happened.

The Necklace

Wind lashed the branches of the trees. The moon, like a diseased face, looked through the racing clouds and then was
hidden again. Edwin Grigg came creeping along the track in
the woods. He stopped when he saw the cottage. Then he
went slowly on.

At the door, he put down his lantern and took out his
knife. It was easy to force his way in. In the kitchen he opened
the lantern and held it up. The place looked poor enough.

There was a snarl and he swung round. The dog had come
out from a dark corner. It was old and shaky but it bared its
teeth, rumbling in its throat.

'You would, would you?' Grigg hissed, as it made a feeble
rush. And he swung the club he carried. The dog fell without
a whimper. He finished it off with his knife.

Then he went to work. He opened drawers and threw their
contents on the floor; he ripped cushions. He forced open a
cupboard. At last he stood still, panting, and growling like
the dog. In a rage, he threw pots on the floor and called.

'Demdike! You know I'm here. You must have heard me.
Come down! Or, I'll come up and drag you down.'

The stairs creaked. A candle flame wavered there. The old
woman was thin with long white hair. The candle shook in
her hand but she spoke bravely.

'What do you want? Who are you?' She saw the dog and
cried out, 'Gyp! Oh, Gyp!' She fell to her knees beside it.

'Never mind that.' Grigg stood over her. 'Where is it?
Where do you keep it hidden?'

'What?' She lifted shaking hands.

'Tell me!' He threatened her with the club. 'The money.'

'I have no money.'

'Liar!' He hit her with his hand. 'I've been down in the village. They talked about you at the inn. You're a woman of strange powers, a white witch. When people are ill, you can cure them. They say animals trust you and are friendly, too. You look after the beasts of the wild. You cure cattle, horses, dogs. Over the years you must have been well paid. You don't go anywhere. You've nobody to spend it on.'

'They don't pay me money. Sometimes I get food. But I don't ask for reward.' She looked down. 'You've killed poor Gyp.' Her voice broke.

'What of it? You'll get the same, if you're not careful. Tell me where you keep the money.'

'There is no money!' she cried.

'Don't lie.' He hit her again. 'Is it upstairs? In the mattress? Where?'

'Nowhere. I have no money.'

'Speak!' He used his fist. 'Where?'

'I can't. I've told the truth.'

'Curse you!' This time he used the club. It caught her on the head. She fell forward over the dog without a sigh. He seized her hair and pulled her up.

'Dead?' he grunted. He let her flop forward again. 'It doesn't matter. I'll find it. Couldn't have left her alive afterwards, anyway.' He stepped over her and climbed the stairs.

When he came down again, he was in a fury. 'Old witch!' He kicked her body. 'I can't find it. Too well hidden.' He turned the old woman on to her back and listened to her heart.

'Just my luck!' he mumbled, as he lifted his head again. 'I've killed her right enough. And time's against me. Ah!'

His eye had been caught by a chain around her neck. It was silver. He tore it off and took it over to the lantern. On the end of the necklace hung a figure made also of silver. It was the figure of an animal, with pointed ears, running.

'Something at least,' he growled. He slipped it into his pocket and picked up his club and lantern. He gave one glance at the bodies on the floor. The dog's eyes were open and seemed to glare at him. With a shrug, he left and, hurrying through the wood, came to the road. At dawn, a wagon, going along, gave him a lift. He was in London late the next day.

It was evening when he came to the lodging-house. It was in a grimy street. The landlord looked at him suspiciously.

'Lodgings?' he asked. 'Can you pay?'

'Of course,' Grigg told him.

'Let's see the colour of your money.'

'Here.' Grigg showed him the necklace.

'That's no good. It's coin I want.'

'I'll be back. I can easy sell this, if you don't want it, and have money left over.' Grigg put it back in his pocket.

'Aye. When you've got money to show you can have a bed and food.' The landlord stepped past him and looked down the street. The lamps were being lit. They gleamed cloudily through the fog.

'What's up?' Grigg asked.

'I thought I saw something out there. You're alone, are you?'

'Yes,' Grigg told him.

'Must have been mistaken.' The landlord went in and closed the door. The street was filling with darkness and wisping fog. Grigg peered into it. There was nothing to be seen. Far off a dog howled. He began to walk through the mean streets that led to the river. At the entrance to the small, dirty shop, he paused, looking back, thinking he had heard something strange. Then he pushed the door, making the bell ring, and went in.

'What've you got this time?' the shopkeeper greeted him.

'This.' Grigg threw the necklace on to the counter. 'How much for it?'

Stern, the shopkeeper, examined it and put it down again.

'Anything else?' he asked.

'No.' Grigg jerked his head at the necklace. 'How much?'

'I won't buy that. Gives me the shivers. Unlucky.'

'Don't talk stupid. It's solid silver, that is.'

'I don't want it. I don't like the look of it—or the feel.'

'You've bought stolen goods before,' Grigg argued.

'I don't want that.'

'It's worth money.'

'Not to me.'

'Damn you, Stern!'

'Shut your mouth and get out,' Stern ordered. 'Take that thing with you. And see that dog of yours doesn't come in here.'

'What dog?' Grigg turned to the window, his mouth open. 'I don't have a dog.'

'Whoever it belongs to—keep it out. Great ugly-looking brute.'

Grigg said no more. He picked up the necklace and went slowly out. In the street he looked up and down. He could see no dog. He could see little in the coiling fog. He needed a bed for the night. He would have to sell the necklace elsewhere. There was a place across the river he could try.

The fog dulled all sound. There was only the noise of his footsteps and the distant hooting of boats. He shivered and hunched his shoulders. The fog grew even thicker and he hurried. It was playing tricks on his eyes, curling before them like strands of long white hair.

Suddenly he stopped dead in his tracks. A dog had howled and another answered it. Eerily, through the dimness, it came again, closer this time.

'Just dogs,' he reassured himself. He went faster after that, all the same, until he halted once more. Another sound had joined that of the wailing boats and the crunch of his steps. What was it in the street at his back? A clicking of claws? A faint padding of feet?

He was about to move on when he gave a cry of fear. In the

light of the street lamp, the beast seemed huge. Was it only a dog? The grey shape stood there, looking at him, its tongue lolling. It had pointed ears and its eyes were pale. It was steathily joined by another and then a third.

Grigg ran with a yell and the wolfish creatures loped after him. A glance behind showed that they were gaining. In his terror and the fog he did not know where he was going. Steps were in front of him and he clattered down them. Before he could stop himself he was ploughing through mud. He had come to the mud-flats by the river where the tide was out.

With a scream he tried to scramble back to the steps. Then he screamed again. Silently, the grey shapes were leaping at him.

It was two boatmen who found him, sprawled there in the mud. They got out of the boat at the river's edge and stood over him.

'Dead?' one asked.

'Yes,' said the other, holding up the lamp. 'His throat's torn out. See.'

'Dogs?' The first one shuddered and turned his eyes away.

'Can't have been.' He lifted the light. 'Look at the mud. There are only his footprints coming down from the steps. No trace of anything else on the mud. No paw marks.'

'Who did it, then?'

'Who knows? Could he have done it himself?'

'Is that possible? You stay here with him. I'll bring the police quick as I can.'

No one came to claim the body and Grigg was buried in a pauper's grave. The necklace was put in a drawer at the police station. But when, weeks later, a curious constable thought to look for it, it had disappeared completely.

Think It Over

What crime besides murder does Edwin Grigg commit?

Why did he kill the dog?

Why does he rip the cushions?

How do you know the old woman is alone in the house?

What was he going to do to the old woman when he found the money? How do you know?

What is the first clue that a dog may be haunting Grigg?

How do you know that Grigg and the shopkeeper had met before?

What kind of animal did Grigg see?

Why were there no animal footprints?

What happened to the necklace?

Do You Know?

Is Grigg clever or stupid? What do you think?

What might the animal on the necklace be?

Why might the landlord have looked at Grigg suspiciously?

Why did the fog look like long white hair?

Who would normally use the steps to the river?

What sort of weather makes you think of ghosts?

What provides the light in a lantern?

About when did people stop using candles to light their houses? Could you put an approximate date to the story?

What is a white witch?

How many kinds of animal have pointed ears? What animals frighten you? Do you dream about them?

What sort of street lamps needed to be lit with a flame?

Using Words

'a mean street' What other words can you use instead of 'mean'?

What do you call a man who buys and sells stolen property?

'The moon *like a diseased face* . . .' and 'The fog . . . curling before them *like strands of long white hair.*' How else could you describe the moon and the fog?

Note the opening sentences of the story. Then write three sentences to grip your readers at the start of your own story about a robbery.

List the words imitating sounds which you find in the story?

'Chortle' comes from two words, 'Chuckle' and 'snort'. What do you call a smoky fog in a city?

'Before he could stop himself, he was ploughing through mud.' Complete the following sentences. They need not have anything to do with the story:

Before the car would start, he had to . . .

He had all the breakfast ready, before his mother . . .

Before he opened the door, he . . .

Before he could get out of the field, the bull . . .

Learn the following spellings: threw seized colour disappear

Write Now

In play form write the conversation two of the villagers might have had on a learning of the old woman's death, or the conversation one of the boatmen might have had later with his wife.

Write a poem called 'A Violent Scene' or 'The Dark, Untidy, Little Shop'.

List three kinds of dog that make good guard dogs and three kinds kept only as pets.

Give an account of how the necklace was lost from the police drawer and what became of it.

Write a story in which you are followed by something strange and frightening.

The Supermarket

The old man knocked on the office door.

'Can I help you?' asked the girl.

'I want to see the man in charge,' said the old man.

'Mr Lewis?'

'If he's the man in charge, I want to see him.'

'Mr Lewis is our chief planning officer.'

'That's him then.'

'I'm afraid he's out. Can I help you?'

'No thank you, I'll wait.'

'He could be several hours. I'm sure I could help.'

'I'll wait, thank you.'

The girl sat him down in the outer office. Later she went to tell the other secretaries about him. 'There's a strange old man waiting to see Mr Lewis. He won't tell me what he wants. He's been there for two hours. He has funny eyes.'

Mr Lewis came hurrying in. 'Has the Mayor called?' he asked.

'No, but there's an old man waiting to see you.'

'Has he an appointment?'

'No.'

'Then I can't see him.'

'But he's been here three hours.'

'I'll see him this afternoon.'

'You'll see me now, please.' The old man was in the doorway. 'It's important.' He fixed Mr Lewis with his eyes.

'Very well, Mr . . .?'

'Earnshaw.'

'Mr Earnshaw. Sit down. Now what is troubling you?'

The old man took a grimy newspaper out of his pocket. 'It's this,' he said. He pointed to a news item.

'The Eastgate Development?' said Mr Lewis.

'You can't build there,' said the old man.

'Why not?'

'You can't.'

'It's not my decision, it's the Council's. They have decided to allow building there for the good of the town.'

'But it's an old burial ground.'

'We know that and we have taken the proper steps with the Church. It's all in order. Nothing for you to worry about.'

'You must not build a supermarket, or anything else.'

'If you wished to object you should have told us months ago.'

'You can't stop it?'

'No.'

'I'll not leave here till you stop it.' The old man sat on the floor.

The police were called. The old man was dragged out. He was taken to the police station but was later allowed to go with a warning.

Mr J. J. Sernberg felt happy. He puffed on his big cigar. The building of his new supermarket was going well. It was in such a splendid position. Trade should be very good.

'There's a man to see you, sir,' called his secretary.

'Who?'

'He won't say.'

'Then I will not see him.'

'You will see me!' The old man had pushed past her into the room to face J. J. Sernberg in his big chair. 'You must stop building that supermarket! Please!'

'Why?' asked a surprised Sernberg.

'It's on a burial ground. You are disturbing the graves.'

'That's all been taken care of. Now I'm sure my secretary can find you a cup of tea.'

'I'll not move from here till you stop.' The old man sat on the floor.

The police were called and the old man was given another warning. But later he was found breaking windows and woodwork on the supermarket site. A doctor was called to the police station. The old man was put in a mental home.

The Eastgate Supermarket was opened by the Mayor. It did splendid business on the first day. Mr Sernberg was delighted.

On the second day, a Tuesday, a Mrs Scroggings was buying a lamb chop for dinner when the meat cleaver leapt from the butcher's hand and floated round in the air. She screamed and ran out of the shop followed by several other screaming women. The butcher fainted. Customers stood fixed to the ground as they saw the floating meat cleaver chopping down tins before finally coming to rest on the counter.

The police were called but they could find no reason for the floating meat cleaver. The shop opened next day, though a new chief butcher had to be found, as the other was ill in bed.

On the second Tuesday a lady was looking at a chicken when the meat cleaver leapt up and knocked off her hat. She fainted. The cleaver, watched by some of the amazed staff, chopped up two chickens into little bits before coming to rest.

The police were called. Sernberg was sent for. All the butchery staff refused to work there any more. Several other members of the staff gave their notice as well. But the next day nothing unusual happened.

At the end of the second week Sernberg looked at his books. Takings at the shop were down. Few people had been in the shop since Tuesday and they were mainly men.

After another incident on the third Tuesday, when the

cheese counter was chopped about by the floating cleaver, fewer people still came in. Sernberg had to work in it himself as two-thirds of the staff had left. His takings at the end of the week showed he was making a big loss.

The grocery manager suggested to Sernberg that a priest should be sent for to exorcize the ghost. This he did quickly but he could give the priest no reasons why the shop might be haunted, except that it was built on an old burial ground. The priest suggested that the meat cleaver should be melted down. Then he conducted a service in the shop.

But this was no good for, on the fourth Tuesday, two knives chased a young girl assistant out of the back door.

Sernberg was desperate. His secretary then reminded him about the old man. He made enquiries and found he was in the local mental hospital.

Sernberg was shown into a small white room. The old man shuffled in with an attendant. Sernberg told him the story. 'Can you help me?' he begged.

'I'm mad,' said the old man. 'They've locked me up. They say I'm barmy. How can a mad man help you?'

Sernberg begged him but the old man just fixed him with his eyes and would say no more.

That night Sernberg could not sleep. He heard many fire engines going to a fire but he did not know it was his own shop till the police rang him.

The shop was completely burnt down. The fireman said some electric cables in the shop had been cut. The police put it down to vandals. What do you think?

Some years later the old man died in the hospital. An attendant going through his papers found an old book. In it was a story of how an Earnshaw had been brutally murdered with a cleaver after an argument in a pub. He had been buried in Eastgate. The day of the murder was a Tuesday.

Think It Over

When do you first know what kind of work is done in Mr Lewis's office?

What did the secretary feel about the old man?

What is Mr Lewis's attitude to the old man at first?

Why was Mr Sernberg pleased about the supermarket?

Why was Earnshaw finally put in a mental home?

What is a cleaver?

Why was the chief butcher in bed?

What happened after the cleaver was destroyed?

Why would the old man not help Sernberg?

How might the cables have been cut?

Did any incidents in the shop happen on Monday or Wednesday? Why?

Do You Know?

Who gives planning permission for building? What sort of permission do you need before you can build anywhere?

What part of the face tells you most about what someone is thinking?

Why might the old man have been late in seeing the newspaper?

How do you feel about building on an old burial ground?

What might the old man have been charged with, the first time he was a nuisance?

How would you describe a typical big-business man?

Was the old man mad? What steps are taken before someone can be put in a mental home?

How would you have felt if you had been an assistant in the shop?

'Sernberg looked at his books.' What would be in his books?

Name two other causes of houses and buildings accidentally catching fire.

Which do you feel is more frightening: ghostly happenings in the day; ghostly happenings at night?

What was the most mysterious thing about the old man?

Using Words

Where might you be if someone asked: 'Have you an appointment?'

And where might you be if they asked: 'Have you got a date?'

'The man in charge.' Can you think of other ways of writing this?

'That's' is short for 'that is'. Shorten these; it is; there is; they are; was not; I will.

How many questions are there in this story? Write six lines of speech about buying something which contains three questions and three answers. (Remember the question marks.)

What kind of ghost makes objects fly about? It begins pol . . .

What is the word used to describe seeing things that do not exist? It begins hal . . .

Give another word for burial ground.

Name two other implements used by a butcher.

'I'll not move from here till you stop.' Complete these sentences. They need not have anything to do with the story:

He could not see till . . .

She was not allowed out till . . .

It rained till . . .

The fire burned till . . .

Till there were four of them there he . . .

'Brutally' is made by adding 'ly' to 'brutal'. That is why it has two l's.

Add 'ly' to these and then learn them: final usual general beautiful

Write Now

Write an account of a similar happening, or write an account of this one for the local paper.

Give an account of how Earnshaw came to know why it was dangerous to build on the burial ground.

List the buildings and places in your town you would like to see preserved.

The police make a plan of the shop. What might it look like?

Write a poem called 'The Old Man in the Churchyard' or 'Building Site' or 'Men who Smoke Cigars'.

In play form write down what one of the assistants tells her husband, or the conversation between Earnshaw and an attendant in the hospital in which Earnshaw reveals his knowledge of the burial ground.

Write a story in which a child or young person tries to convince adults of some oncoming disaster.

Granty

Mr Grant was an old-fashioned kind of teacher. He always wore a suit with a waistcoat, in the right-hand pocket of which was a fob watch. His hair was decidedly short at the back and sides and fluffy-white on top. His brown shoes were always polished immaculately, a relic, it was said, of his army days. In fact he had a thing about shoes: no boy was allowed in his classroom without clean shoes. You could tell which class had him next as boys cleaned their shoes with sleeves, craft aprons, handkerchiefs, anything to hand, to escape his wrath in the doorway of his classroom.

Although at retirement age, he was still regarded as a good teacher. His exam results were outstanding, and those classes not taking exams always worked for him willingly. Yet he always kept at arm's length from his pupils as it were. He called all boys by their surnames and all girls 'Miss'. A Christian name was never known to drop from his lips. Neither did he make any pretence of liking modern fashions or music.

His nickname of Granty was not as insulting as some are and he appeared to have gone through forty years at the same school unaware that anybody ever called him anything except Mr Grant. You could not entirely be sure, of course, because there was always that twinkle in his eye when he spoke of matters concerning himself.

The day of his retirement came. He made a typical speech to the school about honour and was presented with a portable television set which, as the headmaster said, he would now have plenty of time to watch. Those sitting in the front rows could see the twinkle in his eye momentarily turn to tears as he accepted this gift from the school and the PTA.

His lessons that day proceeded in a normal manner. Those pupils who came in expecting a high old time were soon set to work. Some classes were even set work to do in the holidays. His only concession was to run a quiz in his very last period. As each pupil went out that day he shook him or her by the hand. He gave the very last boy to leave his classroom a telling-off about the state of his shirt and also a £5 book token. He then sat at his desk staring at the work on the walls; he was crying.

A cleaner found him two hours later. His head was on the desk. By his side was an empty pill bottle. The hospital was unable to save him.

A new young man, Dylan Rees, fresh from college, took his place. His red hair was long and he had an untrimmed beard. His suit was of faded denim and he wore a cravat inside the collar of a frayed shirt. His suede shoes looked as if he walked permanently in wet sand. The children quickly christened him Catweazle.

'I believe in freedom of communication,' he told them. 'You can write what you like for me; tell me anything you like; ask me anything you like. You will find me very different from Mr Grant.'

The classes did not quite know how to take this at first, though it soon became apparent that Catweazle did not mind talking in class and within a week they had the measure of him. Terry Aubrey was the first to test him: 'What do you have all that fungus on your face for, mate?' he asked. The class waited for his reaction.

'I believe in the basic freedom to dress and look as you like. It harms no one,' replied Mr Rees.

'Why can't we then?' asked Evelyn Dixon.

'I think your school rules are wrong. I shall try to change them.'

There were cries of 'Hooray' and whistles.

'I don't think you should wear scruffy shoes though,' said

Yvonne Hubbard. 'It's not nice.'

'What do you think we call you?' asked Terry Aubrey.

'What do you call me?'

'Catweazle.'

There were shrieks and whistles.

'I don't mind being called Catweazle.' He did not. They had discussed this kind of thing often at college. But the back of his neck pricked in a strange kind of way and his head felt as if held in a tight band.

The bell went. Chairs fell over as the class pushed to get out, eager to impart the news to the incoming class.

'Can we call you Catweazle?' they asked excitedly rushing in for the treat.

'I think we will do some work,' said Mr Rees. The tight band persisted.

But work was the last thing the class intended to do. Mr Rees, though green, was ripe for the picking. A note went round the class from Robert Speed: 'When I blow my whistle all stand up, shout 'Catweazle!' And sit down.'

It worked. The class hugged its sides with glee.

'What did you do that for?' asked Mr Rees. Treat it calmly, he thought.

'It's freedom of expression,' yelled Speed, blowing his whistle. Again the class stood up and shouted, 'Catweazle!' Order was restored by the deputy headmaster who happened to be passing by. He interviewed Mr Rees at four and gave him some words of advice on how to start a teaching career.

At home that night Dylan Rees lay on his bed smoking. I'm right, he thought. I won't change my ideals. Children should be free. Of course, they'll play me up a bit at first, but that'll soon die down when they tire of it.

He was tired. He turned in for an early night but could not sleep. He had the same pricking sensation at the back of his neck and his head felt tight. He felt very cold and began to shiver. His body did not feel like his own but much heavier.

He put the light on and lit a cigarette, but even as he did so his hand pulled it from his mouth and flung it on the floor. He could not understand this; it was as though it was not his own hand. He got up and paced about but his legs felt different. He must be ill. He took three aspirin and managed to doze off.

When he woke he only had a dim memory of what happened the night before. He normally stayed in bed till the last possible moment, did without breakfast, and got to school just on the bell, but now he found himself getting up at six-thirty. He was not quite right, but he could not call himself ill. He looked in the mirror. He did not like what he saw. How could he face children looking like that? He proceeded to shave off his beard and trim his hair. That was better, though he must call in at the hairdresser's after school.

He then started to dress. How had he not noticed the state of his collar before? And where was a tie? And what were these denims doing by his bed? He needed a suit. He took out the one he had been to his brother's wedding in. That was better, and here was a decent tie. But what were his gardening shoes doing here? He found a black pair but there was no polish so he gave them a good rubbing with an old towel.

He then cooked himself bacon and egg, collected up his marking, and set off in good time for the bus. He paused to look in the hall mirror. He stared at his newly shaved face. There was something wrong. He began to feel dizzy and the pricking at the back of his neck started again. Who was he? He sat down.

At that moment his landlady came by. 'Who am I?' he asked.

'You can't play tricks with me. You do look so much better without your beard. You are in good time this morning.'

Yes, he was Dylan Rees, a teacher, and he was going to school. He set off to slouch down the road, hands in pockets, but his back suddenly straightened and his arms swung smartly at his sides.

At school in the staff-room he was ribbed about his beard, but he said nothing, merely smiled with a bit of a twinkle in his eye.

His first class came in like a tube train. 'Where's your beard, then, Catweazle?'

'Get out!,' he yelled. 'Get out and come in again!'

The class looked at him.

'Get out and do it like mice!'

Some of the more timid ones began to move.

'Get out the rest of you, or I'll cane you.'

The others followed except Aubrey.

'Get out, Mr Aubrey,' said Rees.

'Sod off,' said Aubrey, 'you can't cane me.'

Mr Rees leapt at him, grabbed him by his lapels, and pulled him up till he was on his toes. Their faces were half-an-inch apart. 'What did you say, Aubrey?'

'Leggo my jacket.'

'What did you say?'

'I said sod off.'

Mr Rees dropped Aubrey and then hit him full in the mouth. Aubrey sank to the floor. Mr Rees turned to the expectant and hushed class. 'Come in,' he said. The class filed in slowly picking their way past the recumbent Aubrey. 'You, boy! Look at those shoes. You're not coming in here with shoes like that. Get out and clean them.'

'Cor! He's gone like Granty,' said a voice.

'Silence!' God. What was he doing? He had shouted at the class. He had struck a pupil. What should he do? He saw rows of faces looking at him and Aubrey slowly rising from the floor, as if through a mist. His neck pricked. He would teach them, that's what he would do. He would teach them about punctuation. God knows they needed it.

'Give out the files, Moody,' he snapped. 'We are going to do sentence punctuation today.'

'What about our free expression?' asked Evelyn.

'I'll decide what the class does, Miss Dixon. Stop snivelling, Aubrey, and sit up. Sit up all of you.'

All day he taught controlled classes. The deputy head came in to congratulate him at the end of the day. As they talked the pricking in his neck ceased and he started to feel normal. He went to stroke his beard; it was not there. He looked down in amazement at his dress. Then as if awakening from a dream he thought of Aubrey. Surely he had not struck a pupil! He leapt up from his desk. Yes, there were spots of blood on the floor.

'What's the matter?' asked the deputy head. 'Aren't you feeling well?'

'My God!' said Dylan Rees. He ran out of the classroom, and ran and ran through the London streets. A policeman found him exhausted in Trafalgar Square and took him to hospital.

'You will have a new teacher today,' said the deputy head.

'Where's Mr Rees?' asked the class.

'He's ill. He's gone away for a long rest,' said the deputy head.

Think It Over

Name two things about Mr Grant which seem old-fashioned.

Why might Mr Grant cry?

How did he die? What was the reason for his death?

In what ways did Dylan Rees differ from Mr Grant?

Who was the first to sum-up the new teacher?

How would you describe Aubrey's behaviour?

When Mr Rees said that he did not mind how the class behaved, was he telling the truth? How do you know?

What sort of advice, do you think, did the deputy head give Mr Rees?

How did Mr Grant's early morning routine differ from Mr Rees's?

When is Dylan Rees's body first taken over?
In what ways did Dylan Rees become like Mr Grant?
When did the class recognise what had happened to Mr Rees?
What would you say caused Dylan Rees to run out of school?
Where might Mr Rees have his long rest?

Do You Know?

What is a fob watch?
Why should polished shoes remind people of the army? What other thing about Mr Grant might tell you he had been a soldier?
At what age do teachers retire?
What do you feel about the use of Christian names by a teacher?
How do your grandparents spend their retirement?
What do you feel about Mr Grant's last day?
Which teacher would you have preferred?
Do you believe in freedom to dress as you like?
What is fungus?
Where else besides London do you find underground railways?
Have you ever felt not yourself? If so what was it like?
Why is Trafalgar Square so called?
Where do you think Mr Rees came from?

Using Words

Write down seven things you own in a sentence beginning: 'I own . . .' How should it be punctuated?
What other titles besides Mr and Mrs do you know which are in regular use? What do you feel about titles?
Make a list of nicknames of people in your class. Why do people have nicknames?

'Order was restored by the deputy headmaster who happened to be passing by.'
Complete these sentences. They need not have anything to do with the story:
I once saw a man who . . .
I used to know a girl who . . .
There were many unusual people in the crowd who . . .
I know where they can find the boy who . . .
Who was in the room . . .
How would you address: a headmaster, a doctor, a bishop, a mayor, the Queen or King?
Recumbent means: injured; unhappy; lying down; angry; unconscious? Write down the word you think is nearest in meaning and then check with your dictionary.
When Terry Aubrey calls Rees 'mate' it is insulting. Who could you call 'mate' without being insulting?
'Within a week they had the measure of him.' 'Mr Rees, though green, was ripe for the picking.' Write these sentences more simply.
'His first class came in like a tube train.' Give two other comparisons suggesting noise and speed without using the idea of trains.
'He was ribbed about his beard.' Give another word for 'ribbed'.
How do you feel about swearing? Is swearing ever justified?
Learn these spellings: always   shriek   calmly   cigarette

Write Now

Describe someone whom you feel is typically old-fashioned.
Write a story in which some person is taken over by someone else; it could be a vampire story.
Write a poem called 'The Bad Class'.
In play form write down a conversation between a mother and father whose son or daughter has been acting in a

peculiar manner, or write the conversation Mr Rees had with his doctor about the hauntings.

List things you think are important about personal appearance.

Suicide Rock

Out in the bay the old man was fishing. He looked at the cliff-top and looked away. Then he looked again. He took out a pair of field-glasses and trained them on the spot. He watched for a moment. Then he put the glasses down quickly and began to row for the shore. He had been watching a young man.

The young man, Mike Bruce, sat down on the cliff-top and bit his nails. He was very pale and his face was lined with worry. He was sweating. It was a bright, cloudless day but it was not warm enough for that. He took his hand away from his mouth. It trembled. He covered his eyes and groaned. He couldn't go on any more.

He had been angry enough not to care when his parents had thrown him out. After that, drifting, he had got into a bad crowd. Now he was sick of the habits he had picked up and sick of living off social security. Being with Tina had made things better. But Tina had finished with him. He wouldn't see her again. Why had he come to this place? He had slept in bus shelters for the last two nights. He might have found a better place to stay but what did it matter? The worst of all was feeling so worthless. He was worthless to others and worthless to himself. He had felt that deeply, walking alone along the front through the cheerful holiday crowd. There was not one face he had known. He was sick of it all and sick of being Michael Bruce. Perhaps that was why he had come here. He had kept seeing the cliff all day. It was high and steep. Now all he had to do was to walk twenty paces and jump. There were rocks at the foot. A long fall, a sharp pain and then—nothing. Blackness. Peace.

'Lovely day.'

Mike jumped and swung round. He had been so sunk in misery that he had not noticed the girl's approach. She smiled and he forgot the utter drabness of his life for a moment, feeling friendly towards her. Maybe that was because she was a bit of a misfit like he was. Though she was young and pretty, her clothes were odd rather than trendy.

'Makes you glad to be alive,' she went on. Her voice was soft and calm, almost a whisper. 'Look at that sky. And the light on the water. And the freshness of the air. I'm often here. There aren't too many days in one's life like this, are there? See those sea-pinks? I love flowers like that.'

'Do you? Yes,' he said. It did not seem a very clever remark. But she seemed so strange. And yet—she was attractive. She made him feel different, not so hopeless. 'I hadn't noticed the day,' he told her.

'On the map, this place is called Banner Headland,' she said. 'The locals call it Suicide Cliff. Over the years quite a lot of people have ended their lives by jumping off here.'

He looked at her suspiciously. Had she guessed? Was she hinting to warn him? He hated being interfered with. But she was looking out to sea. She did not seem to be talking to him, more to herself.

'There was a girl not so long ago,' she went on. 'She felt lost—deserted. No one to turn to. She came up here. It was a week day in autumn. Not a day like this. Not many people about. She threw herself off. If she'd waited—perhaps she could have found help.' She shivered. 'It was—silly.'

She turned and looked at him. 'It's a dreadful place,' she told him seriously. 'Just go and look.'

Five minutes ago, if he had walked towards the edge, he would not have stopped. Now, everything was changed. It was just a cliff-top, an ordinary place. She had changed things for him.

'All right,' he said and even smiled. He walked to the edge and looked down. She was right. It was a terrible drop. The tide was nearly in but the grey rocks stuck up like broken teeth. No one could survive that fall. He shuddered and turned away.

When he saw that the girl had gone, he felt a sharp pang of disappointment. So, on her side, it had been just an idle chat. She must have got up just as he walked to the cliff edge and wandered off, disappearing round that shelter up there. Maybe she had gone down the steps to the promenade and then the beach beyond.

'Hey!' he called, feeling it was no use. 'Wait a bit!' He had liked her very much and not just because she had changed his mood. She had been such a strange mixture, quiet and somehow sad but sympathetic; wise and older than her years.

He ran up past the shelter and clattered down the steps. His eyes searched the promenade; then he ran down on to the beach. Some children were playing, a man was gathering up deck chairs. A fisherman was pulling a boat up on to the sand. There was no sign of the girl.

Then he noticed that the old man with the boat was staring at him. Mike gazed back, puzzled. The old man glanced away. Then he seemed to make up his mind. He looked at Mike again and came determinedly up.

'Excuse me,' he said. 'You don't look too well. Let me get you a cup of tea. There's a stall just up on the promenade. You look as if you've had a bit of a rough time of it lately.'

'What?' Mike did feel cold and a bit dizzy. He could imagine how he looked.

'Let me explain,' the old man went on, noticing his hesitation. 'I saw you from the boat. Up there, on your own. A lot of people have killed themselves there. I'm not cracked.' He put out a hand as if to stop Mike from saying something. 'There was a girl. She had this affair with an older man. It's some years back. Her parents threw her out. Then the man deserted her. She had a baby. It died. She was desperate, all on her own. When we knew, when we came back from abroad, me and the wife would have taken her in, helped her.

She was my niece, you see. Don't think I'm being daft about this, being rude,' he rushed on. 'I saw you from out at sea, through the glasses. You looked so desperate. I got this peculiar feeling. I rowed back at once. I kept having a look at you. I was watching you all the time. You seemed so alone. Alone up there all the time.'

Mike looked at him a little dazedly. He passed a hand over his brow. 'Yes,' he said. 'I would like a cup of tea. Someone to talk to. Thanks very much.'

'Come on then, lad.' The old man took his arm. Mike hestitated. He stood there gazing at nothing while the old man waited.

'All alone, up there? For the whole of the time?' Mike murmured. 'Yes. Yes. I suppose I was.'

Think It Over

When do you first know that Mike Bruce is nervous?
How did he feel when his parents threw him out?
What was the name of his girl friend? What happened to her?
What was the first strange thing he noticed about the girl who
    spoke to him?
How did Mike feel about the girl?
How did she make him change his mind?
Where did she go?
What did the old man notice about Mike?
What did Mike appreciate about the old man's offer beside
    the cup of tea?

Do You Know?

What kind of people use field-glasses?
What inshore fish might the old man have been fishing for?
Why did he quickly row for the shore?

How do you react when you are worried?

What kind of people had Mike been mixing with?

Why should he be living off social security?

In what other places do 'down-and-outs' sleep beside bus shelters?

Have you ever felt worthless? What made you so?

Why had the cheerful holiday crowd made Mike feel worse?

Are most people reluctant to talk to strangers? How do you feel? Why?

What society helps people who feel like committing suicide? People in trouble can telephone them. The name of the society begins with an 'S'.

How do you feel about heights? How would you have felt looking down from the cliff top?

Have you ever had a strange feeling that something was about to happen? Were you right?

Had Mike really been alone on the cliff top?

Using Words

'He stood there gazing at nothing while the old man waited.' Complete these sentences. They need not have anything to do with the story.

He stood by the garden gate while . . .

The girl filed her nails while . . .

While it was raining . . .

While the news was on the television . . .

While he looked . . .

Read the first paragraph. Then write down four separate things a person does in making a cup of tea. Use 'then' only once in your sentences.

'A bright cloudless day'. Write down the opposite of this.

What is the word for feeling dizzy when in a high place? It begins ver . . .

'But the grey rocks stuck up like broken teeth.' How else

could you have written the *underlined* phrase?

'I'm not cracked.' How many ways can you think of to say this?

'A bit of a misfit.' Give five other words you can make by adding 'mis' to an existing word (lead—mislead).

'Hey!' What do you say to stop a stranger if you wish to be polite? What does the old man say?

'Come on then, lad.' The old man uses the word 'lad' because he does not know Mike's name. Give other words you might use in a similar situation.

Learn these spellings: clothes (there is an 'e' in this) different people broken

Write Now

Write a story about someone strange you may have met.

Write a poem called 'Loneliness' or 'Looking Out to Sea'.

Describe the clothes that were fashionable three years ago. Sketch them if you like.

Write a story about two lovers who were drowned, or one called 'Was it Suicide—or Murder?'

In play form write either the conversation between Mike and the old man afterwards, or the dialogue between a man threatening to jump off a high building and a policeman trying to talk him out of it.

Bed but no Breakfast

John and Mark cycled down the road. They had been sent there by the warden of the youth hostel. The hostel had been full. 'Try Drum Road,' said the warden. 'There are plenty of bed and breakfast places down there.'

They were on a cycling holiday in Scotland. They had not booked at any hostel but had been lucky at getting in until this one. Now they were forced to try and find accommodation for the night and it was getting late.

The first three cottages were full and could take no more visitors. They were beginning to wonder where they would spend the night when they saw a battered notice on a broken gate-post: '—ed and —kfast', it said. They could see no cottage but a track led between tall trees. A half moon was beginning to show through the top branches.

'It looks a bit creepy,' said Mark.

'Rubbish!' said John. 'Let's try it, otherwise we'll be sleeping under the stars. I'm dog-tired.'

The track wound through the trees for about two hundred yards. The trees formed a tunnel in the coming darkness. Suddenly they came upon a house. It was large and in very bad repair. Creeper grew over most of it, even the roof in places. There were shutters at the windows which creaked in the wind.

'Do you think anyone lives here?' asked Mark.

'Let's knock and see,' said John. 'It's our last chance.' He lifted up a heavy metal knocker. Its sound echoed into the house. They stood listening to the rustling creeper and creaking shutters.

'There's no one here,' said Mark. 'Let's go.'

Suddenly a light flickered through a red glass panel over the top of the door and footsteps slowly shuffled their way towards them. A bolt was shot back. The door opened.

Before them stood a man with a white beard so hairy that his face seemed all eyes. He was holding an oil lamp. 'What do you want?' he barked. The mouth was small and the beard was tobacco-stained round it. He had no teeth.

'We're looking for bed and breakfast,' said John.

'You should go to the hostel.'

'It's full,' said John.

'Well, I have one room. Come in.'

The boys followed him in. The hall was full of heavy furniture covered with dust.

'Stay here. I'll get ye a lamp.' The old man shuffled off.

'We can't stay here; it's filthy,' said Mark.

'We'll just have to put up with it,' replied John. 'It's a roof.'

The old man returned. In the flickering of the oil lamp they could see that his back was bent, almost hunch-backed. 'Follow me.'

They went up a flight of stairs, the old man breathing heavily. He opened a door on the first landing. 'This is the only room I have prepared. Tak'it or leave it.'

The room was big. The wallpaper was peeling off. In one corner was a large brass bedstead.

'We'll take it,' said John.

'I'll leave you to it, then. Breakfast at eight downstairs. Oh!' The old man turned in the doorway. 'If she comes tak' no notice of her. Just tak' no notice of her.' He shut the door.

'Who's she?' asked Mark.

'Perhaps it's some other lodger,' said John, 'who's noisy, or something. Let's get to bed.'

The boys washed in cold water from a jug and then undressed for bed. The bed seemed to have more than one mattress on it and was high up from the floor.

'It's damp,' said Mark, shivering. 'God knows what my

mother would say.'

'It'd be damper outside,' said John. 'It'll soon warm up. There seem enough blankets on it.'

'The whole house smells damp to me.' He turned on his side. 'Shall I leave the light on?'

'Why?'

'I might want to get up.'

'There's a chamber pot under the bed. I kicked it getting in.'

'Can I have the matches then?'

'Here you are.' John passed them over. He was soon alseep.

Mark could not get off. He lay, listening to John's breathing and the window shutter creaking in the wind. But he must have dropped off in the end, for he suddenly woke with a start. It was no noise that woke him but what felt like a pain in the back, as though something was digging in to him. His back was also numbed with an intense cold. At first he thought that the blankets had fallen off but they were still heavy on him. The bed, with the two of them in it, should have been very warm by now. Was he ill? Had he got a chill from the damp? He started to shiver. He fumbled for the matches to light the lamp but could not find them. He lay staring up into the darkness, wondering if he should wake John. An owl hooted. The shutter bumped gently on the window. Then slowly he became aware that . . . no . . . it was not possible. He held his breath. Yes . . . there seemed to be two people breathing in the room besides himself. He searched the darkness and tried, with shaking arm, to find the matches. It must be his imagination. Perhaps he had a fever. 'John!' he called. 'John!'

'What's the matter?' mumbled John.

'There's something else in this room.' As he touched John, who was further away in the bed than he thought, the intense cold went through his arm.

'Nonsense.'

'We must put the light on.'

'If you must.'

'I can't find the matches.'

'I've got another pack somewhere. Gosh, it's cold in this bed, isn't it? Here you are.'

With trembling fingers Mark lit the lamp. Then he shrieked, so much that John got out of bed with him.

'Look!'

Although both boys had got out of bed, there was a depression in the pillow, as if a head was resting on it and the blankets instead of being flat were all plumped up as if over a body. From the bed came a sound of snoring.

Mark opened his mouth but no further sound came.

'My God!' said John. They held each other like small children.

Then the door handle turned and the door slowly opened. The old man stood framed in the cool light of the oil lamp. 'Is she bothering you, then?' he asked.

'The bed,' stammered John.

'It's only her,' breathed the old man. 'I told you to tak' no notice. Get away with you, wifey. Away with you, you silly old hag.'

The snoring stopped and the bedclothes dropped down while the pillow plumped up.

'She'll no' be back,' said the old man. 'She canna stand being spoken to harshly. You can tak' ye rest with no more worry. Goodnight.'

The two boys looked at each other. 'I could never get in that bed again,' said John.

Mark's speech had returned. 'Never mind the bed. I can't stay in this room a minute longer.'

Hurriedly, with one eye on the bed, the boys got dressed. They flung two pound notes down on the chest-of-drawers, picked up their rucksacks, crept down the stairs, unbolted the front door and pedalled hard down the track to the main road.

As the light of dawn came up they could be seen heading back in the direction of England.

Think It Over

What does the notice and the gatepost suggest about the place
    where they are to stay?
Where does the story start to get creepy?
What kind of a night was it?
What clues are there that the house is old?
When do we first know that the housekeeper is old?
Why does the oil lamp flicker? What can be creepy about it?
Which of the boys is more particular about where he stays?
What two modern amenities does the room lack?
Which of the two boys is more nervous?
What is the first odd thing the old man says?
What was digging into Mark's back?
Why might he not have been able to find the matches?
Is the old man a ghost too? What do you think?
Why might an old woman be haunting the place?

Do You Know?

What is a youth hostel? Can anybody stay in one?
How much does it cost to stay the night in a hostel?
How much might you have to pay for bed and breakfast in a
    hotel?
What is another word for 'accommodation'?
Name two kinds of creeper growing on houses.
What is the creepiest house you have ever seen?
What creaks in your house?
What in tobacco causes the stain?

Why can long bushy beards be mysterious?
Where does dust come from?
What makes wallpaper peel off walls?
What is the most unusual room you have seen?
When did you last feel afraid in bed?
Do you know a ghost story in which the temperature was a
   part of the story?
What would you find most frightening about Mark's situa-
   tion when he wakes up?
Could you have slept in the bed again? Why?

Using Words

Did you know what '-ed and -kfast' meant? Can you give
   these in full: '-o -passing' '-ep -ff -e -rass'?
What is the most unusual notice you have seen? We like the
   one—'Toilets 15 Miles'.
'At first he thought that the blankets had fallen off.' Complete
   these sentences. They need not have anything to do with
   the story:
   This is the hotel that . . .
   I had a feeling that . . .
   I want you to know that . . .
   The only reason I can think of is that . . .
   This is the ghost that . . .
How would you describe a half moon? The half moon was
   like . . .
'dog-tired.' Why do we say 'dog-tired'? How many other
   common phrases can you think of that mention animals?
'She'll no' be back.' How would it have been written if the
   man was English?
'chest-of-drawers' has hyphens in it to make it one thing. Put
   hyphens in these words: bed sock   foot bridge   knee cap
Now find three of your own in the dictionary. Remember
   they must name things.

Write Now

Write a story about a spooky house or describe the creepiest house you know.

Write a poem called 'The Thing in the Bed', or 'Travel by Night', or 'Things That Keep You Awake at Night'.

What happened to the old woman? Why did she want to sleep in that bed? Tell the story.

List the things you would need to take on a cycling or youth hostelling holiday.

List the things you think need doing in the old man's house. Also list what needs doing in your house.

In play form Mark tells his mother what happened.

Roughly copy out a map of Scotland. Then plan a tour to see: The Cairngorms, Loch Ness, Skye, Edinburgh.

The Walking Dead

The clock ticks. It is the loudest sound in the house. It is very late.

Last night they took Susan away. Since then I have not eaten or slept. I shall leave this as a warning. I cannot stay here. This house reminds me of terrible things. It is still full of what I saw and the thing I had to do. Be warned. Leave the things of darkness well alone.

Let it warn the village people, too. I have no reason to like them. But they helped last night.

They never liked us. They were afraid of my grandmother. They did not speak to my parents. I think they feared Susan. They said the women of our family were witches. They said we used black magic. They were polite to Susan because they were afraid. But they laughed at me because my speech is strange and my legs are twisted.

Susan and I have lived alone for the past five years. It was harder for my sister than for me. I do not want much from life. Susan did. She wanted excitement. She wanted marriage and children. I could not expect it. Who would marry me? She had many black moods. She had a strong will and she grew angry with life.

Then, for a while, it changed. I remember the day when Michael walked up the path. It was autumn and the leaves were red and gold. He stopped as Susan came round from the back of the house. They stared at each other.

77

'I'm looking for a room,' he said.

'You're not from the village, are you?' she asked.

'No.' He smiled. The wind moved his black hair. He looked a happy young man. Even I could see that he was handsome.

'A room?' Susan said.

'Yes,' he said. 'I've got a job on one of the fishing boats. I'm working for a man called Wallace. I shall need somewhere to stay. Do you know anywhere?'

'We have a room,' Susan said. 'Do you want to look at it?'

'Please,' he said.

'Come in.'

They went upstairs but I could see that it was already settled. Susan liked him. So did I. He liked her, too. Anyone could see that.

Michael stayed with us and he stayed in the village. Wallace was not a bad man to work for, he said. After a week, he and Susan were in love. It could not be hidden. They did not want to hide it. It went very deep with Susan.

'I don't know how I lived before he came,' she said once to me. 'I don't know how I could live without him.' She always felt things very strongly. The vicar felt like the rest of the villagers. But he had to agree to marry them. It would be in three weeks time. Michael did not mind what the villlage thought. He was too interested in Susan to care. And I have never seen Susan so happy.

But it did not last. Terror came instead. You get some rough weather in our parts in autumn. And the sea runs strongly. A man who falls overboard in a storm is not often seen again. And the tides do not wash up the bodies. Mr Wallace came to tell us in the morning.

'Michael!' That was all Susan said.

'He went overboard last night,' Wallace said.

'Where?' I asked.

'Far out,' he said. 'In the middle of that storm. You must have heard it.'

'I was awake,' I said. 'You searched?'

'We searched for over an hour. We searched again this morning at first light. There was no sign. There was nothing on the beach. I'm sorry. I liked him. There was nothing we could do. There'll be the usual service in church on Sunday. Just a service. No burial. We'll never find the body again. I'm sure of that.'

Susan just stared at him. Her face was dead white and she looked suddenly very much older. It had killed some part of her, too. 'I'm sorry,' Mr Wallace said again and went away. I took Susan inside. She said nothing all that day. She sat in a chair as if she were in another world.

At night I lit the lamps and sat with her.

'I must have him back,' she said suddenly. 'I can't bear it.'

'He can never come back,' I told her.

'He must,' she said.

'The dead can never come back,' I said.

'There are ways,' she said. 'I will find them.'

'Don't think about it,' I said. 'Let the dead rest.'

'I can't,' she said. She looked wild. I said no more. I did not want to make her angry.

But my blood ran cold when I saw her with the book. I knew where it came from. It had been in the loft. It had belonged to grandmother, the one the village called the witch. Mother would not let anyone touch it. But she would not destroy it either. It was as if she was afraid of the old book. Neither Susan nor I had touched it until then.

'Put it back!' I said.

'It shows me the way.' She gave a secret, wicked smile.

'It's evil.'

'I don't care.'

'Put it back.'

'You can't make me. I tell you—I will have Michael back.'

She was right. I could not make her. She was stronger than me. She took the book everywhere with her. At night she used it as a pillow. I could not get it to destroy it. She started going out nearly every night and returning just before the morning. Twice I followed her. The first time she went far into the country. She was gathering herbs by moonlight. She went too far for my legs. I could not keep up.

The second time she went to the graveyard. I hid and watched. She began to dig. I could not see what she took from the ground. I left her alone then. But when she came home, I argued with her again.

'What you are doing is terrible,' I said.

'You can think what you like,' she told me. 'It makes no difference. I know now what I have to do.'

'I watched you in the graveyard,' I said. 'Stop this. Susan! Stop before it's too late.'

'Neither you nor the devil himself will stop me.'

'It's the devil I'm thinking of,' I said. 'You are giving yourself to him. Aren't you afraid?'

'I'm afraid of nothing. And I won't care about the power of the devil, if I have Michael back,' she said.

It was no use. I tried again and again to argue with her. But, in the end, she stopped answering anything I said.

It was not until last night that she spoke to me. Her smile twisted her face. 'It is finished,' she said. 'He will come tonight.'

'He can't,' I said. 'Michael is dead—drowned. The dead do not rise up.'

'Michael will.' She gave that horrid smile. 'I have made the charm and said the words. We shall see at midnight.'

The house was very still as it is now. She had set out little bowls on the window sill. The window was open and they had liquid in them. It sent a strong scent out into the night. It was dark with only a thin moon in the sky. She had put out all the lamps except one. I could see a few stars. The first stroke of midnight sounded from the church.

Susan stood at the window and cried out. The words were in a strange language that I did not understand. The hair crawled on my neck. Three times she cried out. Then we waited.

'He is coming,' she whispered at last. I, too, could hear the sounds. They were slow and dragging. They were first in the lane and then, louder, on the path. 'Michael!' Susan cried. Her eyes blazed with excitement. She took up the lamp and rushed to the door. The shuffling steps had stopped outside. She flung the door open and held the lamp high. 'Michael!' she cried again. Then she screamed.

The thing outside was not Michael any more. His swollen hands hung at his sides. His black hair hung wetly across the empty holes of his eyes. Fish had eaten at his face. I stood behind her and I saw. From his swollen mouth came noises. She screamed and fell to the floor. The lamp fell with her. The thing that had been Michael stood, swaying.

I hobbled into the other room and flung the bowls and the evil liquid into the night. Susan's screams filled the house. I can hear them now. When I went back the thing had fallen on to the path. I could still hear its noises.

I brought men from the village. They took Susan away. Her screams had become groans and she knew no one. But, before I brought them, I dragged the flopping thing on the path away. I got a spade and a sharp stake from the shed. I buried it deep. I put the stake in its heart. It can lie quiet there now. Evil will not awaken it again.

They told me Susan would recover. But they are wrong. Her evil has made her mad. She will always be mad now. You may think from this tale that I am mad, too. But you will be wrong. Be warned. Do not deal with darkness as Susan did. Do not call men from beyond the grave. The walking dead are neither young nor handsome. Not when they have been ten days drowned.

Think It Over

How do you know that it is night and the house is very quiet at the beginning of the story?
What is the man's reason for writing it?
Why might his speech be strange? Why could he not expect marriage or children?
Why did the villagers fear the family?
When do you first know that Susan and Michael are attracted to each other?
What was the vicar worried about in the marriage?
Why could they not recover Michael's body?
What kind of book was it that Susan found?
What changes took place in her after Michael's death?
What did she want the herbs for?
Why could her brother not stop her doing what she did?
Why did she scream?
Do you think she could ever recover from her madness? Why?

Do You Know?

What makes the loudest sound in your house at night?
What do you understand by 'the things of darkness'?
Who has the better character, Susan or her brother? Why?
What sort of job, do you think, is the most dangerous?

82

In what part of the country might the story take place? Why?

When do you get the roughest weather at sea?

What causes tides?

Why might Susan and Michael have had to wait three weeks before they got married?

Why might the mother not have destroyed the book in the loft?

What bodily symptoms do you get when you are afraid or have had a bad shock?

Using Words

Another word for black magic is sorc . . .

'My blood ran cold'. How many other ways can you think of saying this?

The word for a black mood begins depr . . . . What is it?

Describe autumn in a sentence. You could begin, 'Autumn is like . . .'

'A thin moon is like . . .'. How would you describe a new moon?

Look again at how the speech punctuation is done. Then write three questions and three answers in speech.

'Neither Susan nor I touched it till then.' Find the other neither . . . nor sentence in the story and write one of your own.

What words does 'up' go with? For example, keep up, sit up.

'I knew where it came from'. Complete the following sentences. They need not have anything to do with the story:

I told the farmer where . . .

Jones reported to the officer where . . .

The police directed the cars to where . . .

We asked the old man where . . .

Write Now

Give an account of any other story like this you have read or any film you may have seen.

Write a description of the most horrible thing you can imagine.

In play form, write a conversation some of the villagers might have had about Susan.

Write a story set at the seaside. It could be that you were there one day on holiday when something came out of the sea.

Draw a picture from the story.

Aunt Maud

'Going out?' asked Mrs Shenton. She kept the guest house.

'Just for a walk,' said Miss Mimms.

'I wouldn't go through the woods.'

'The woods?'

'Not at nightfall.'

'No? Why not?'

'It could be dangerous. They're near the sea. And the fence by the cliff is broken down.'

'I see. I'll be careful.'

'It's not just being careful, my dear,' said Mrs Shenton. 'I wouldn't go in them at all.'

'Goodbye,' said Miss Mimms, smiling sweetly.

The first star was in the sky. An evening mist covered the ground. She felt quite excited. It was the first time she had felt free in years. But it was not just getting rid of Aunty Maud. There was more to it than that.

She could think of Aunty Maud now. She could remember that fat, wrinkled face and the soft voice that went on and on. She would be resting by the fire. Then would come the knock on the ceiling. She would run upstairs. 'Read to me, dear,' Aunty Maud would say. And Miss Mimms would read to her.

She would be on her way downstairs. 'Ellen!' Aunty Maud would call. Miss Mimms would run back. 'Draw the curtains back, dear,' Aunty Maud would say. 'I like to look at the night. It's friendly.' And Miss Mimms would draw the curtains back. 'Don't go,' Aunty Maud would say. 'Sit by my bed. Stay with me. I like you with me.' And Miss Mimms would sit with her.

Then, Miss Mimms would be going to sleep. Aunty Maud would call her. Miss Mimms would go in. 'I can't sleep,' Aunty Maud would say. 'Sit in that chair and chat.'

'What shall I chat about?' Miss Mimms would object. 'I'm tired.'

'Don't chat then. Just sit. I want company. I want you with me. You must stay with me always, Ellen. We must not be separated. You are all I have in this world. Stay with me.' And Miss Mimms would stay. Sometimes far into the night. Sometimes until the dawn came. Then Aunty Maud would sleep. She often seemed strangely wide awake at night.

Miss Mimms had to stay with Aunty Maud. Aunty Maud had all the money. Miss Mimms came to hate Aunty Maud's bedroom and the house and Aunty Maud herself. But she could do nothing. She was at the old woman's mercy.

And that was not the worst of it. Aunty Maud kept to her bed. But she did not seem really ill. Sometimes, it seemed to Miss Mimms that her aunt could live for ever. And Miss Mimms, herself, was growing old. She could see it every day in the mirror. Miss Mimms wanted romance before it was too late. But what chance did she have of meeting handsome men? What chance did she have of meeting any men at all? Not with Aunt Maud calling on her services at all hours. Aunt Maud wanted her all the time. Aunt Maud wanted to possess her completely.

So Miss Mimms had made her plan. It was not easy. It depended on luck. But Miss Mimms had had luck. Once—just once—Aunt Maud had needed the doctor. It was for nothing, really. She had had a bad stomach. The doctor had come and left her some powder. It was to be taken in water.

Miss Mimms had spoken to him afterwards. She had explained things to him. Because her aunt slept badly, she had to stay awake, too. Couldn't he give them both some sleeping pills? The doctor had written out a prescription. Then her aunt had complained that the stomach powder tasted bad. So Miss Mimms gave it to her in strong, sweet fruit juice. It disguised the taste of the stomach powder. It disguised the taste of the sleeping pills, too. Because of the sour taste of the stomach powder, Aunty Maud would drink up all her fruit juice as quickly as she could. Miss Mimms crushed up most of the sleeping pills and gave them to her aunt. Aunt Maud had not suspected. Not until the end. She had stared in a terrible way at Miss Mimms then. But by then she could not speak.

The doctor may have suspected. But he did nothing. No one wanted to examine the body. And Miss Mimms got all the money. She was free. She was free to get away and find romance. So she had chosen 'The Laurels', Mrs Shenton's guest house.

At first, it had seemed a mistake. There were no men staying there. In fact, Miss Mimms was the only guest. It was, after all, autumn. And the country round about was odd and lonely. Miss Mimms had been quite disappointed. At least, she had been disappointed until today. Miss Mimms gave a little skip and forgot all about Aunt Maud.

Today she had seen the dark and handsome stranger. And he had not only seen her, he had been interested in her. Just before tea, she had gone for a walk. In the distance had been a wood. It was obviously the one Mrs Shenton had talked about. A man had come out of the wood. Miss Mimms had stopped and looked. The man had looked back. He was tall, in a long coat. Miss Mimms could not see his face very clearly. But her imagination told her it was handsome. He had waved at her. He had called something. It sounded like 'Ellen!'. But he could not have known her name. Then he had gone back into the wood. She might have followed him then. But she had not known many men. As a person she was shy. It was nearly teatime. He might not have been waving at her. For many reasons she had gone back to the guest house.

Then she had been annoyed with herself. She had been silly. It had been her first chance of romance and she had not taken it. It had not taken long to decide. She would go back. She was almost at the woods now.

She gave an excited squeak and her hand flew to her lips. The man was there again. Again he waved. Miss Mimms began to hurry. But he went back into the woods. 'Wait!' called Miss Mimms. But he did not hear her.

The path led in among bushes and trees. It was quite dark in there. But not too dark. She could see him, a little way ahead. 'Wait!' she called again, and hurried after.

She had to dodge branches. Thorns caught at her stockings and her hands. She was no nearer to the man. She caught glimpses of him as he went along. Miss Mimms lost all caution. She knew it was silly. It was not ladylike at all. She could not help it. She called loudly, 'Wait! Oh, wait!' and she ran.

He had stopped. He was about to turn and wait. 'So silly, but—' she gasped as she tripped. She stretched out her hands to him to save herself.

But there was nothing there to touch. She was out of the woods in the evening light. The cliff at her feet fell away. The sands, a hundred feet below, rushed up to meet her.

Miss Mimms came to herself. Beside her lay her body, its neck strangely twisted. 'Forgive me for the little trick I played, my dear,' said a voice. 'I forgave you for yours.' Miss Mimms did not need to turn. She knew what was behind her. There was a ghostly touch on Miss Mimms' ghostly shoulder. 'I was lonely without you. Now we can be together for ever and ever,' said Aunt Maud.

Think It Over

When do you first know how Miss Mimms feels about her
    aunt?
When was Aunt Maud most awake?
Why could Miss Mimms not leave her aunt?
What were the irritating things about Aunt Maud?

Why did Miss Mimms want to be free of her aunt? What caused Miss Mimms to make her plan?

What sign of her suspicions did Aunt Maud give just before she died?

Why had Miss Mimms been disappointed with the guest house at first?

Why did Miss Mimms not follow the man when he waved to her the first time?

Who was the stranger?

Do You Know?

What hint is there at the start as to how Miss Mimms might meet her death?

What is the coastline in the story like?

Why might Aunt Maud have wanted Miss Mimms' company all the time?

Why did the stranger not wait for Miss Mimms to catch up?

Why would Miss Mimms not be able to escape from Aunt Maud again?

Have your parents ever had to look after a sick relative? How did they feel?

What must you be careful not to do with sleeping pills?

What clue in the story suggests autumn?

Do you ever have dreams in which you are following someone or being followed? If so, what happens?

What should you not do on cliffs?

What do you find most frightening about the story?

Using Words

What is the word for the illness when you cannot sleep? Ins
. . .

Make a list of words of your own which describe Aunt Maud. Can you think of five?

'The countryside around was odd.' Give three words, any of which could be used instead of 'odd'.

'Because her aunt slept badly, she had to stay awake, too.' Complete these sentences. They need not have anything to do with the story.

Because the . . . , he . . .

Because Mr Morris . . . , his assistants . . .

He arrived very late because the train . . .

Because April was . . . , they . . .

The quarrel between the two men became an open fight because one of them . . .

Short sentences are used for the effect of tension and suspense. Where in this story have they been used for that? Write about six short sentences of your own about a person who is alone in the upstairs room of an empty house when something moves on the floor below, comes upstairs and along the landing.

Write Now

In play form write the conversation Mrs Shenton has with the investigating policeman about Miss Mimms' behaviour.

What clever ways of murdering people have you seen on television? Make a list.

As a detective, make a plan of the grounds of Mrs Shenton's guest house, the woods, the cliffs and the sea.

Describe the room of an invalid.

Write a poem called 'The Beach at Dusk' or 'The Darkness in the Wood'.

Give an account of a strange old man or woman.